# John Cena

## ELBOW GREASE

### vs.

# MOTOZILLA

# John Cena

# Elbow Grease vs. Motozilla

I'm back, baby!

Illustrated by Howard McWilliam

Random House 🏠 New York

Every weekend, the four stars of the Demolition Derby gathered in the center of the arena to start the show.

Some fans liked Tank best because he was big and strong.

Some fans liked Flash best because he was fast and cool.

Some fans liked Pinball best because he was smart and skilled.

Other fans liked Crash best because
he was brave (and maybe a little bit crazy).

Hey, I have fans, too!

Elbow Grease had fans, too: his four big brothers and his best friend, Mel the mechanic.

ELBOW GREASE IS THE BEST!

No one else knew that during practice, Elbow Grease was the star of the show.

When the truck brothers were training, Elbow Grease worked twice as hard as anyone else, and he never gave up, no matter how tired, dented, or frustrated he was.

What if I'm all three at the same time?

Elbow Grease inspired Tank, Flash, Pinball, and Crash to work harder and improve their monster truck skills.

I learned how to swivel my rockets to improve my speed!

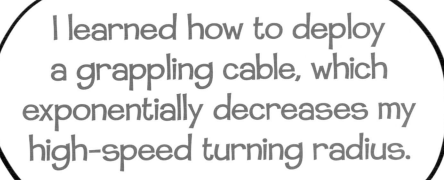

I learned how to deploy a grappling cable, which exponentially decreases my high-speed turning radius.

I learned how to pop my pistons to improve my vertical.

I learned to smash cars with my butt.

Sometimes Elbow Grease wished he was the best at something. He was afraid that no matter how hard he worked, he might never be as strong as Tank, as fast as Flash, as smart as Pinball, or as daring as Crash.

But, 'Bo, you're the best at getting better.

Elbow Grease wasn't sure that was something a fan would paint on a sign.

ELBOW GREASE IS BEST AT STEADY IMPROVEMENT

Couldn't I just be most handsome instead?

It was true. Even their hero, Big Wheels McGee, couldn't defeat the dreaded monster machine.

Ow-y kazow-y . . .

Elbow Grease decided it was time for Motozilla to lose. But how?

To defeat Motozilla, a truck would need:

It would be impossible to find a truck with all of those qualities!

That's when he had a flash of inspiration.

Elbow Grease explained his plan to his brothers.

They decided to trust their little brother and try his big plan. Elbow Grease asked Mel for help, and she got busy in her workshop.

Then they headed back to the arena to practice . . . and practice . . . and practice. . . .

On the night of the big match, the arena was totally packed. Fireworks exploded in the sky, and the lights went dark.

Motozilla had giant claw hands.
Motozilla had smashing spring feet.
Motozilla had a chain-saw whip tail.
As if that weren't enough, Motozilla
could breathe scorching-hot fire.

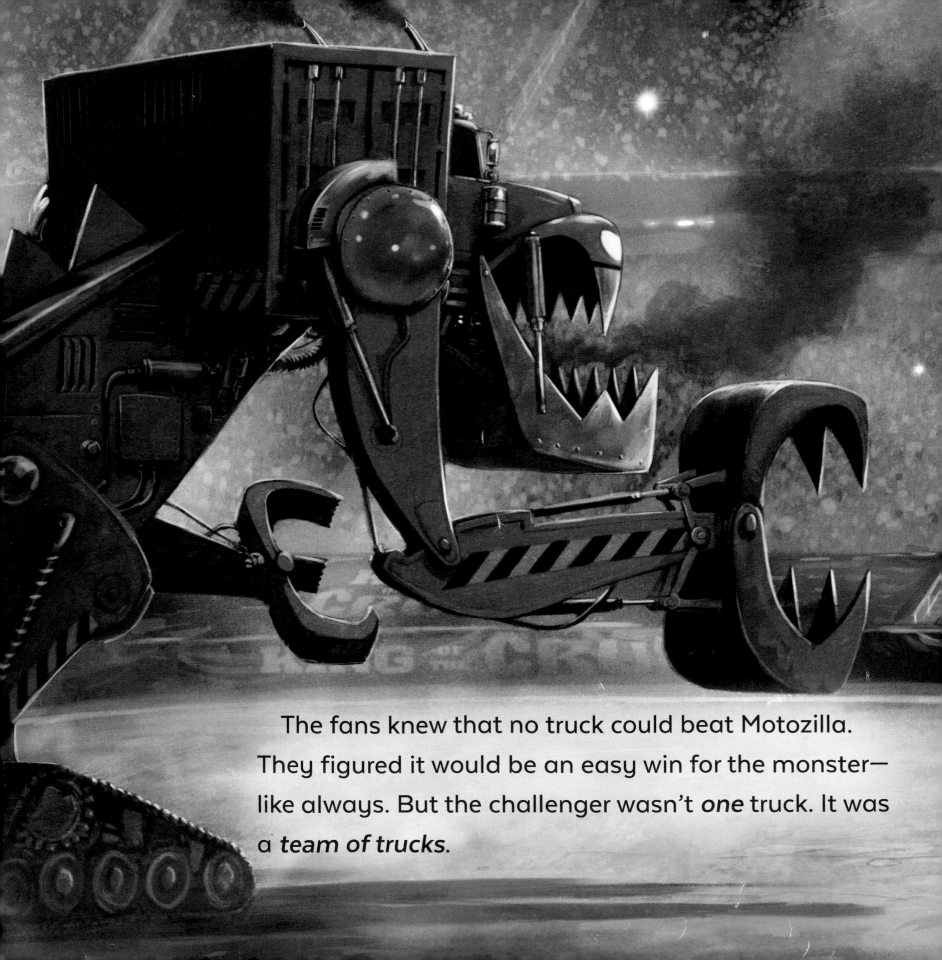

The fans knew that no truck could beat Motozilla. They figured it would be an easy win for the monster— like always. But the challenger wasn't *one* truck. It was a *team of trucks*.

Motozilla tried to claw at the team,
but Tank smashed the claw in half.

Motozilla tried to smash the team,
but Pinball outmaneuvered the springs.

Motozilla tried to saw the team, but Flash rocketed away from the whipping tail.

Through it all, Elbow Grease led the way.

The monster was tough and the brothers were exhausted, but Elbow Grease wouldn't let them give up. He flashed his lights and sounded his siren.

Never give up!

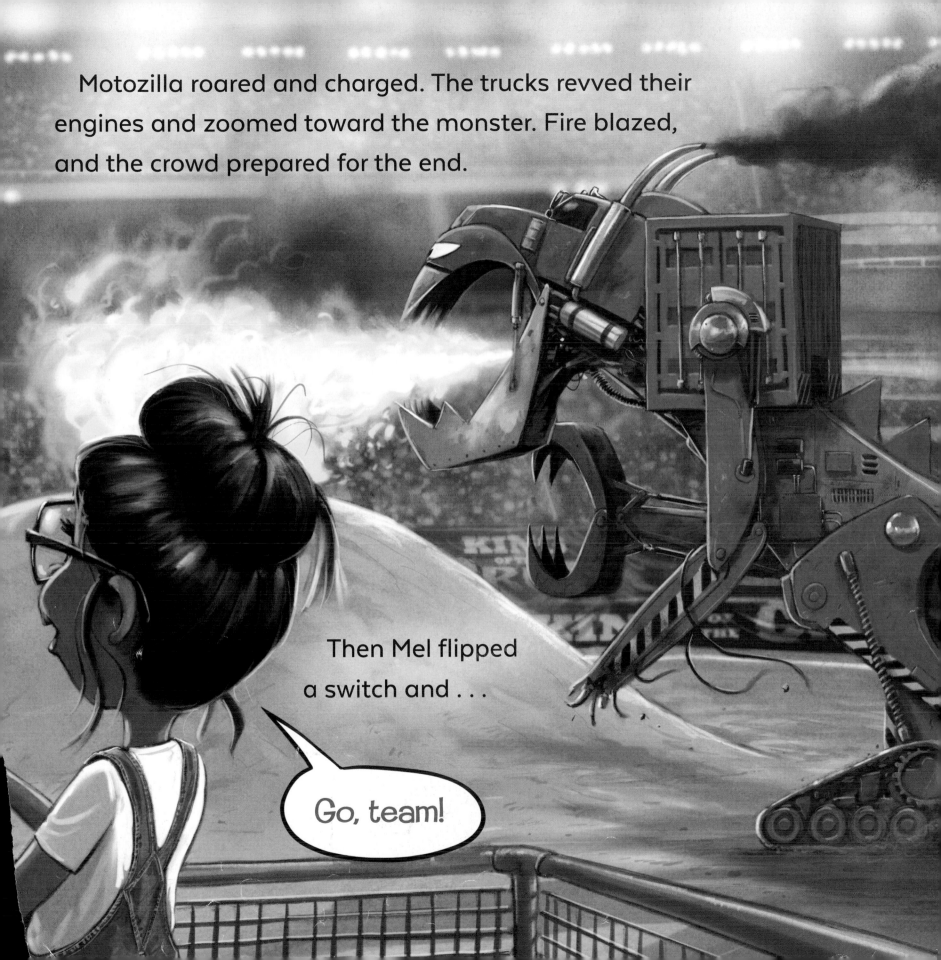

It wasn't easy, and it definitely hurt a lot, but they did it. They had worked together as a team and done something amazing. Something none of them could have done alone—no matter how strong, or fast, or smart, or brave.

After that day, the fans at the Demolition Derby started making different signs.

# THE END

All rights reserved. Published in the United States by Random House Children's Books, a division of Penguin Random House LLC, New York.
Random House and the colophon are registered trademarks of Penguin Random House LLC.
Visit us on the Web! rhcbooks.com
Educators and librarians, for a variety of teaching tools, visit us at RHTeachersLibrarians.com
Library of Congress Cataloging-in-Publication Data is available upon request.
ISBN 978-1-5247-7353-3 (trade) — ISBN 978-1-5247-7354-0 (lib. bdg.) — ISBN 978-1-5247-7355-7 (ebook)
Book design by Roberta Ludlow
MANUFACTURED IN CHINA
10 9 8 7 6 5 4 3 2 1
First Edition